This book belongs to:

_____

_____

_____

First published 2010 by Walker Books Ltd
87 Vauxhall Walk, London SE11 5HJ

This edition published 2011

4 6 8 10 9 7 5

© 2010 Lucy Cousins
Lucy Cousins font © 2010 Lucy Cousins

The author/illustrator has asserted her moral rights.

Illustrated in the style of Lucy Cousins by King Rollo Films Ltd

Maisy™. Maisy is a registered trademark of Walker Books Ltd, London.

Printed in China

British Library Cataloguing in Publication Data:
a catalogue record for this book is
available from the British Library

ISBN 978-1-4063-2951-3

www.walker.co.uk

Maisy Goes on Holiday

Lucy Cousins

WALKER BOOKS

AND SUBSIDIARIES

LONDON • BOSTON • SYDNEY • AUCKLAND

The holidays have come at last!
Oooh! How exciting!
Maisy is packing her blue bag
to go to the seaside.
Sunhat, camera, books.
What else will she need?

Maisy's taking the train and Cyril is coming too. There he is, buying the tickets. The station is so busy today.

The train pulls
away from the platform.

Maisy does some colouring.
Cyril chooses some snacks.

Everyone looks for their tickets when the conductor comes.

Look! Nearly there!

Can you see the sea?

At the hotel Maisy and Panda bounce on the bed. Then it's time to unpack and go to...

the beach!

Splish! Cyril likes to paddle.

There's so much to do on the beach –

collect shells,

build
castles,

run about and
play for hours
and hours.

At the beach café,
Maisy has an ice cream

and Cyril has a
fruit juice special.

Then they write postcards.
Cyril writes to Charlie. Maisy
writes to her friend Dotty.
"Our first day at the seaside
was lovely," she tells her.

And it's lovely staying in the hotel.

Sleep well, Maisy.
Sleep well, Cyril.

Have a happy holiday!